Good Night, Little Blue Truck

Alice Schertle

Illustrated in the style of

Jill McElmurry

by John Joseph

Houghton Mifflin Harcourt

Boston   New York

Bumpity-bump!
Down the road
came Little Blue Truck
with good friend Toad.

Thunder **crashing!**
Lightning **flashing!**

Two good friends
were homeward dashing.

Such a wet and stormy night!
Their warm garage was a welcome sight.

In they went and shut the door,
but it wasn't very long before—

"Maaaaa!" said Goat. "Please, Little Blue, can I come in here with Toad and you?"

"**Cluck!**" said Hen. "It's wet outside!
I need a nice safe place to hide!"

"Honk!" said Goose. "Don't care for lightning! Stormy nights are a little bit frightening!"

"**Moo!**" said Cow. "Can I come in too?
I feel safer here with you!"

"**Quack!**" said Duck. "There's quite a crowd!
Can I squeeze in? Are ducks allowed?"

"**Oink!**" said Pig. "Is there room for me?
I'm cold and wet as I can be!"

"Beep-beep-beep!" said Little Blue.
"There's room for you, and you, and you.
   Everybody gather round.
   Thunder's such a *grumbly* sound!"

"Clouds bump and tumble in the sky,
but here inside we're warm and dry,
and all the thirsty plants below
will get a drink to help them grow!"

Close to Blue—
over and under—
they listened to
the rain and thunder.

Duck said, loud as he could quack it,
"THUNDER'S JUST A NOISY RACKET!"

"BOOM!" said Goat. "It isn't scary.
I was not afraid . . . not *very*."

"Just a noise," said Pig. "No wonder,
I'm not scared of a little thunder."

After a while
the clouds blew on.
The night was still.
The storm was gone.

Goat said, "We feel better, Blue.
It's easy to be brave with you."
Pig said, "I feel sleepy now."
"Let's all head for home," said Cow.

"Beep!" said Blue. "Just hop inside.
All aboard for the bedtime ride!"

The rain had stopped
and way up high
the moon was a smile
in a starry sky.

"Good night, Pig. Here's your pen."

"Good night, Duck."

"Good night, Hen."

"Good night, Goat. You're home now."

"Good night, Goose."

"Good night, Cow."

Horn went "Beep!"
Engine purred.
Friendliest sounds
you ever heard.

Blue and Toad drove home together,
two good friends in any weather.

Toad lay down on his own small bed.
"**Croak!** Good night, Little Blue," he said.

Blue gave one small sleepy "Beep."
Then Little Blue Truck fell fast asleep.

To Jen, Drew, Spence, Dylan, Kate, John, Marrie, and Aaron —A.S.

For Shauna and Jack, my shelter on the stormy days —J.J.